AL E. GATOR

Visits Croakerhochen

By Bill Dix

For his daughter, Dorothy Lynne

Originally Written and Illustrated in 1968
Edited for Publication in 2010

ISBN: 1452893160
ISBN-13: 9781452893167

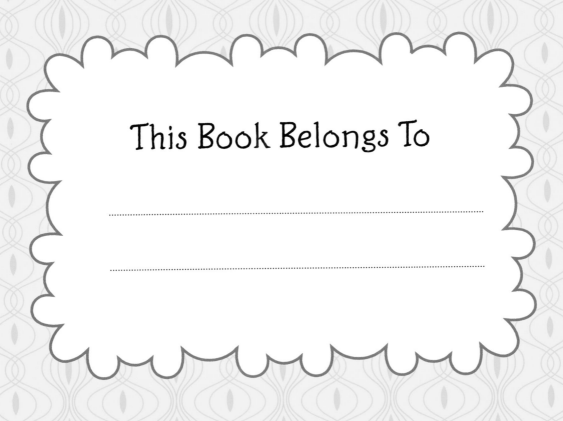

This Book Belongs To

....

....

Forward

In 1968, while serving in the United States Army during the Vietnam War, my father, Bill Dix, wrote and illustrated this book for me, his then six-year-old daughter. Knowing that war is not an easily understood concept for a child, he wrote a beautiful story about frogs, toads, and alligators to explain why he had to go away, for so long.

Written on an old typewriter, illustrated with felt tip pens and magic markers, and bound together with tape and old metal fasteners, this book was sent to my grandmother's house in East Landsdowne, Pennsylvania, where I lived with my mother, one-year-old brother, and grandparents. As a child, I can still remember how excited I was to receive a gift from my dad, sent all the way from Vietnam, specially for me! My mother would read it to me over and over again, every time invoking sheer delight!

"Al E. Gator Visits Croakerhochen" is the story of a young frog, named Arthur, and his family, whose swamp is visited by a predator named, Al E. Gator. AL would lurk in the waters every day hoping to have a "fine frog feast."

The tale goes on to explain how Arthur's father, with the help of many brave frogs and toads, lures Al away, so the swamp can once again be a safe place for the "townsfrog" to work and the children to play "leap-people" and "catch flies."

Although the book remained locked away in my parent's safe for over 30 years, the family often commented that "it should be published." I asked my father if he would allow me to take the book with the intention of updating, editing and ultimately publishing it. He gave me his blessing. That was 5 years ago.

On May 4th, 2010, my father was diagnosed with lymphoma, a blood cancer. It was at that moment that publishing this book became a priority. Without the knowledge of either parent, I intend to present a completely published version of "Al E. Gator Visits Croakerhochen" to my father and mother at their surprise 50th wedding anniversary party, planned for October, 2010. I can think of no better gift to give the man who has been an inspiration and a tremendous role model to our family.

At present Dad is undergoing treatment for stage one, non-Hodgkin's lymphoma. Though the effects of chemotherapy and radiation have been challenging, a full recovery is expected.

I have the utmost respect and admiration for my father. I am thankful for his service to our country; for all that he has done for our family, and especially for this book, which has always been so dear to my heart. I love you, Dad.

Daniel Toad saw Al passing through Wortington

Al E. Gator
Visits Croakerhochen

Once upon a time there was a young frog named Arthur. He lived with his mommy and daddy in a once-friendly swamp, called Croakerhochen. Arthur remembered the good times when he could swim and hop and play leap-people with the other frog children, but times had changed in Croakerhochen. Now poor Arthur and all the other frogs were scared to leave their homes, because a great big monster had come to Croakerhochen. His name was Al E. Gator, and he loved to eat frogs.

Al E. Gator heard that lots of frogs lived in the swamps of Croakerhochen, although he had never seen one. The frogs had Daniel Toad, the Mayor of Wortington, to thank for that. He had seen Al passing through his town on the way to Croakerhochen, and, because he was a smart toad, knew what the gator's intentions were. He quickly called Arthur's daddy to warn him that Al E. Gator was coming his way. Arthur's dad, who happened to be the Mayor of Croakerhochen, told all of the frogs to cover their homes with lily pads and stay inside so that Al E. Gator would not know that they were there.

Al E. Gator would swim around Croakerhochen all day looking for frogs; each day coming a little closer to their hidden homes. He was sure they were there, somewhere, and he really wanted a "frog in his throat!" After all, he was getting tired of pork and beans.

One day as Al was searching for frogs, he was closing in on Arthur's house. Luckily, he did not find Arthur and his family, but before he left, Arthur heard him mumble, "I will not leave this swamp until I have a fine frog dinner." Arthur wanted to cry, but he didn't dare make a sound. Al E. Gator knew that sooner or later the frogs would have to come out. His plan was to lurk in the swamp and wait for the frogs to leave their pads. Such a mean, mean gator!

As days passed into weeks, the frogs became increasingly frightened, and they were running out of food. Even the mommy frogs with little tadpoles, were finding it harder and harder to feed their babies. The adult frogs of Croakerhochen couldn't work, the little frog children couldn't play outside, and worst of all, everyone knew that it wouldn't be much longer until Al E. Gator would find them. Something had to be done to rid the swamp of "Big Bad Al!"

Closer and closer Al got to the frogs home

As Mayor of Croakerhochen, Arthur's daddy thought and thought. Finally one night, long after Arthur was in bed, he came up with a plan. It was dangerous, and he would need help from all the brave frog men and women of Croakerhochen. He would also need the help of Daniel Toad and several townstoads of Wortington.

That night Arthur's daddy called every pad in Croakerhochen requesting the bravest, strongest frogs come to a meeting at his house very early the next morning, before Al E. Gator awoke. He told them that, although his plan was dangerous and would take them away from home for a long time, the swamps of Croakerhochen would once again be safe. The men knew that Arthur's daddy was a very wise frog and all of them quickly agreed to be there.

Arthur's daddy also called his friend, Daniel Toad, and asked if he would help rid the swamp of Al E. Gator. Daniel agreed to help as well.

"I will need you to gather ten of your very fastest toads and hop all the way down to Gatorville, Mississippi," said Arthur's daddy. "I have heard that gators there are friendly. They eat no meat, including frogs and toads!"

"I've never heard of such a thing!" exclaimed Daniel Toad.

"I have it on good authority," said Arthur's daddy. "When you get there look for a lonesome girl gator, named Crocka Doll. If we can lure Mr. Gator there, I believe he may stay."

Even though Gatorville was over 1,000 miles away, Daniel Toad agreed to lead his toads there. He knew that toads can hop much faster than frogs can swim and there was no time to waste.

After much planning and many calls in the night, Arthur's daddy finally went to bed hoping to get some sleep, but morning came quickly. Arthur was awakened by the knocking of the first frog to arrive. It was Arthur's Uncle Guy. Soon there was another frog, then another, until 147 brave, strong, frogs crowded into Arthur's living room. Then Arthur's daddy revealed his plan.

"We will all swim to the middle of our swamp, here in Croakerhochen, and call Mr. Al E Gator until he sees us. When he does, he will try to catch us, but we will be ready. We'll swim away from him and away from Croakerhochen."

"Mr. Gator is a mean customer and very fast in the water," Arthur's daddy continued, "so we will have to swim faster or he will surely eat us. If we stay just ahead of him, he will follow us. We must swim through creeks, streams, rivers, ponds and other swamps all the way to Gatorville, Mississippi. This is where a very special girl gator lives. When we get there, I think he will decide to stay, because I have a plan to keep him there. Only after he makes the decision to stay, can we return home to our families knowing that our swamp will be a safe place to live once again."

The brave frogs understood what they had to do to save the swamp, but first they had to say good-bye to their families. Arthur and his mommy started crying because they knew all of the dangers awaiting Arthur's daddy and how much they would miss him. All over Croakerhochen it was the same. Everyone was sad as they said their good-byes.

Arthur's daddy gave Arthur and his mommy a final kiss goodbye. The army of frogs then headed to the middle of Croakerhochen swamp and waited. Behind each lily pad, the children and their families watched, fearing for the lives of their loved ones.

The army of frogs headed toward the middle of the swamp

As Al E. Gator was opening his usual morning can of pork and beans, he looked out across the swamp and couldn't believe his eyes! Frogs! Lots of them! He immediately slithered into the water for what he thought would be a frog feast, but it was not to be. The frogs were ready for him. As Al approached, they quickly swam away and headed for the big river that led away from Croakerhochen, south toward Gatorville, Mississippi.

Soon the frogs and Al were out of sight, and for the first time in three months, the frogs of Croakerhochen could safely leave their pads. Frogs from nearby Tinicum swamp came to Croakerhocken to help return things to normal. The mommies and daddies left behind went back to work. Arthur and his friends played leap-people and caught flies again. For the moment, the frogs of Croakerhochen were happy.

It didn't take long, however, for them to realize that their loved ones would be gone for a long time, and were in danger every minute that Al was chasing them. Arthur's father and all of the other brave men and women were in everybody's thoughts and prayers.

Meanwhile, the army of frogs, led by Arthur's daddy, kept just a little ahead of Al. It had been two days, and they were all very tired. "How long can these frogs last?" Al muttered. "I am getting tired of chasing them and will have to give up if I don't catch them soon." With that, he gave one more burst of speed, but the frogs managed to stay ahead of him.

Finally, Al E. Gator could stay awake no longer and decided to sleep, thinking that he would let the frogs go. But the frogs did not go. The frogs slept too, taking turns, so that someone was always awake to watch Al.

When morning came, Al was pleasantly surprised to see the frogs still there, and the chase was on again. For weeks and weeks, Al chased those frogs, who always managed to stay just a little bit ahead. Wherever and whenever Al would stop to rest, so did the frogs. There were times when he almost caught them, but he never did.

Back in Croakerhochen, everyone missed the frogs that were leading Al away. The children didn't completely understand why it was taking so long for their mommies and daddies to come home. Yes, the swamp was safe again, but things were not the same without them. As more and more time went by, everyone worried about their safety and if they would ever return.

9

Arthur continued to go to school and play with his friends, but he missed his daddy all the time. He could see how much his mommy missed him too, but all they could do was wait.

Now Arthur had a wise grandfather, named Pop-Pop Croak. Pop-Pop Croak was too old to go on the mission with the younger, stronger frogs, but because he was wise, all of the frogs put their faith in his words. Pop-Pop Croak would say, "I have a fine son who will return home safely one day with the other frogs and toads, and Mr. Gator will bother us no more."

Hearing his grandpa talk about how brave his daddy was made Arthur feel happy and proud. Talks with Pop-Pop gave him faith that his dad would be home soon. Whenever Arthur felt very sad, he would sit on Pop-Pop's lap as the old croaker would tell him stories about Arthur's daddy as a young tadpole and how they would play baseball and "catch flies." This always made Arthur feel better.

Pop Pop Croak

Meanwhile Daniel Toad and his knot of toads had arrived at Gatorville, Mississippi, and found it to be a friendly town where gators, frogs and toads lived in peace. The toads were not afraid of the gators there, because they knew about their vegetarian lifestyle. Daniel explained how Al E. Gator was terrorizing the swamps of Croakerhochen, and asked a friendly gator, if he knew where the lonely croc, named Crocka Doll, lived. The gator told Daniel, and the toads hopped off to meet her, just as Arthur's daddy had planned.

When the toads arrived at Crocka's house, they were surprised to see how pretty she was. She was a "living doll," which is probably how she got her name. Though a bit shy, she was very nice. The toads told Crocka about Al E. Gator and Arthur's daddy's plan. Crocka Doll was eager to help. She invited the toads in as they waited for Arthur's daddy and all of the other frogs to arrive.

It had been 75 days since the chase began and the frogs were very tired, as was Al. Just as they were getting ready to rest for the night, Gatorville came into view. A very weary army of frogs was glad to be there. They were also glad it was night, and the gators were sleeping. Even though they had heard that Gatorville was full of nice gators that didn't eat frogs, one can never be too sure.

12

Crocka Doll

Daniel Toad was waiting patiently along the bank in front of Crocka's house, when he saw Arthur's Daddy and his troop swimming toward him. With Al following closely behind, Arthur's dad gave the signal to follow Daniel Toad to Crocka Doll's house.

As the frogs followed, Al was gaining on them. Quickly all 147 frogs jumped through the door behind Daniel. And just as the last frog was safely inside Crocka's house, they slammed and locked the door, smashing, Al's long snout, as he cried, "Ouch! That hurt!"

Al was confused and upset as he waited outside, muttering "Why is someone protecting these frogs?" He decided to wait and see.

Inside Crocka was preparing a good, hot meal for the hungry and exhausted frogs. Since leaving Croakerhochen, they were only able to eat what they could "catch on the fly." Whatever Crocka was making sure smelled good. As Arthur's Daddy watched the croc cooking, he thought, "I really think my plan will work!"

After the frogs and toads finished their meal of black-eyed peas, macaroni and cheese, corn on the cob and biscuits, they thanked Crocka and quickly fell asleep. They were so very tired after their long trip.

Crocka did not sleep. She peaked out the window at Al. She thought to herself, "That poor, confused scoundrel; all alone without a friend in the world. I bet if I got to know him, he wouldn't be so mean. And after he tastes some good cooking, he won't want to chase those poor little frogs anymore." As she turned away from the window to go to bed, one more thought came to her. Under her breath, she whispered, "He's kind of cute!"

Crocka awoke early the next morning and prepared a great, big gator bowl, full of hot grits for the frogs and toads. After they ate and thanked Crocka, she asked them all to hide in her cellar because she was going to invite Mr. Gator in for some breakfast. The frogs and toads quickly retreated.

After they were safely hidden, Crocka went to her front door, and for the first time, Al and Crocka met. Al could not believe his eyes. She was so beautiful, but it was she who was protecting the frogs.

Without even saying "Hello," Al yelled, "After I chased those frogs for such a long time, I never thought another gator would protect them."

Crocka smiled and in her soft, southern drawl said, "Won't you come in and have some breakfast?"

"You bet I will!" Al huffed. "Frog Stew!"

"No, not frog stew," Crocka said, putting her hand on his chest to stop his approach. "I have prepared something special for you."

Al, still angry, grumbled, "We'll see about that!" and pushed his way through the door.

"You mind your manners, Mr. Gator. I much prefer a gentleman," she said with a calming smile.

Just as Al was about to respond, he caught a whiff of the breakfast that Crocka had prepared for him and he stopped in his tracks. "What is that magnificent smell?" he asked.

"I made you a cheese omelet, hash browns and muffins with jam. Are you hungry?" Crocka asked.

"Starving!" Al replied.

When he saw the breakfast Crocka had made just for him, he forgot all about the frogs and suddenly put on his best behavior, as he pulled out Crocka's chair.

"Now that is more like it! Why thank you Mr. Gator," she said as she batted her eyes.

The frogs were listening intently in the cellar and noticed that Al E. Gator did not seem so mean anymore. In fact, the more time he spent with Crocka, the nicer he sounded. Arthur's father was very happy, because he knew that Al liked Crocka, and Crocka liked Al, too.

Upstairs, Al was really enjoying his breakfast. He hadn't had a good home-cooked meal since he was a boy gator, many years ago, and he had no idea that vegetarian food could taste so good! He thought to himself, "I could get used to this!"

After breakfast, Al and Crocka just sat and talked, and by this time the frogs had figured out what Arthur's daddy had been planning all along. Arthur's daddy saw how lonely Al was. He knew that all he needed to do was find him a mate. Once these two lonely soles found each other, it wouldn't take long for them to realize that a nice girl gator that was also a good cook, might make Al want to settle down and stop chasing frogs.

A few frogs peaked out of the cellar door, and it was plain to see that Al and Crocka were falling in love and would be very happy together. Al would never come back to Croakerhochen. He would stay in Gatorville with Crocka, settle down and probably raise a few baby gators.

The frogs rested all day in Crocka's cellar. Once Al fell asleep Crocka told the frogs and toads that it was safe to come out. Arthur's daddy and Daniel Toad thanked Crocka Doll for her hospitality, and then began their long excursion from Gatorville, Mississippi, back to Croakerhochen, Pennsylvania.

Just as they got outside of town, Arthur's Uncle Guy had an idea, which all of the frogs and toads agreed was a good one. They would build a boat and sail home.

With all 147 frogs and 11 toads working together, the boat was finished within two days and they sailed merrily home. It took them just fifteen days to get back. On the way, they stopped at Wortington, and dropped the toads off, thanking them for their help.

You can imagine how happy everyone was when they saw that boat sail into the swamp! All of the frogs leaped with excitement as they welcomed home their heroes. Parades of happy frogs hopped through the swamps, fireworks lit the sky, and joy spread through Croakerhochen.

Arthur's daddy was the first to spring from the boat. As soon as Arthur saw him he hopped into his arms, grinning from ear to ear. Yes, everyone was happy, but no one was as happy and proud as Arthur, because it was his Daddy who had saved the once again happy swamp of Croakerhochen.

The End

Arthur with his mommy and daddy happy again

7177080R0

Made in the USA
Charleston, SC
31 January 2011